*I*t was a night to remember! Eight-year-old Princess Anastasia waved to her mother as her father—Nicholas, Czar of Imperial Russia— whirled her across the ballroom floor.

Tonight they celebrated a special anniversary. Anastasia's family, the Romanovs, had ruled Russia for 300 years.

When the dance ended, Anastasia ran to the arms of her grandmother, the Dowager Empress Marie. Her grandmother planned to go home to Paris soon, but Anastasia begged her not to go.

Marie held out a tiny jeweled music box. She used a small key to wind it, and it played a gentle melody.

"It's our lullaby!" Anastasia gasped in delight.

Marie handed the key to Anastasia. "You can play it at night before you go to sleep and pretend that I am singing it."

Engraved on the key were the words "Together in Paris."

"Oh, thank you, Grandmama!" Anastasia cried.

Suddenly, the orchestra stopped playing. The laughter faded. An uninvited guest cast a dark shadow across the ballroom floor.

Rasputin—the evil holy man! He stood before the Czar and uttered a curse: "I will not rest until I see the end of the Romanov line—forever!"

With that threat, Rasputin disappeared. Shaken, the guests departed. The party was over.

That night, a crowd of angry demonstrators gathered outside the palace. They chanted: "Death to the Czar! Let the people rule!"

Once again, Rasputin appeared; he raised his reliquary, an ornate vial on a golden chain. Evil minions imprisoned inside the reliquary squirmed against the glass. "Fulfill my curse," Rasputin commanded.

A flash of light from the reliquary smashed open the palace gates. The hordes of revolutionaries surged onto the palace grounds. They toppled the statue of the Czar. They threw rocks and bricks through the elegant palace windows.

Servants roused the Romanovs from their sleep. They ran for their lives in nightgowns and slippers.

Anastasia stopped suddenly. "My music box!" Her long red curls whirled around her as she ran back to her room.

"Anastasia!" her grandmother cried. "Come back!"

But Anastasia would not leave her precious music box behind.

$A$s Marie reached her granddaughter's room, she heard heavy boots pounding along the polished floor of the upstairs hallway.

All of a sudden, a section of the wall slid open—the door to a secret passageway! Out stepped a young servant boy named Dimitri. "This way," he urged them, "out through the servants' quarters!"

He shoved them inside. The music box tumbled from Anastasia's hands.

Dimitri slammed the secret panel and shielded it with his body just as several angry men stormed into the room. "Where are they, boy?" one man demanded.

Dimitri's eyes flashed in defiance. "They're not here."

The man struck the boy and hurried out to search the rest of the palace.

Sprawled on the floor, Dimitri reached for Anastasia's music box and tucked it inside his shirt.

The palace erupted in flames as Anastasia and Marie ran into the dark night. Seeing them escape, Rasputin's bat, Bartok, flew off to tell his master.

As Anastasia and her grandmother slipped and slid across an ice-covered river, Rasputin jumped from a bridge and grabbed Anastasia by the ankles.

With a shriek, Anastasia broke free as the swift current of the river sucked Rasputin into the freezing, dark waters.

Bartok swooped down and captured the glowing reliquary.

At the edge of St. Petersburg, Anastasia and her grandmother struggled to board a train. As the engine started down the tracks, strong hands pulled Marie aboard.

But Anastasia's hand slipped from her grandmother's grasp. She stumbled and fell. Her head struck the cobblestone street and she lay still.

"Anastasia!" Marie screamed.

Would she ever see her beloved granddaughter again?

𝒯en years later, the people of St. Petersburg stood in long lines just to buy a crust of bread. The revolutionaries had promised them a new government and a better life without the Czar. But most were poorer—and hungrier—than before.

"Have you heard?" a woman gossiped to her neighbor. "The Czar's youngest daughter—Anastasia—might still be alive!"

The Dowager Empress Marie, who lived in Paris, had offered a reward of 10 million rubles to anyone who could find her!

*D*imitri—now a handsome young man—had cooked up a plan with a gray-haired former aristocrat named Vladimir. They were searching for a girl—an actress perhaps—to *pretend* to be Anastasia. They would dress her up, teach her what to say, then take her to Paris. The old Empress would be easy to fool, and they would walk away rich men!

If only they could find the right girl to play the part. . . .

Out in the countryside, a girl in tattered clothes stood at the gate of the orphanage where she'd lived for ten years.

"I've got you a job in the fish factory," the headmistress snapped. "It's time you went to work—and be grateful, too!"

"Huh!" Anya muttered. "Grateful to get *away*!" As she hurried off, she fingered the key that hung from a chain around her neck. It was her only clue to her past. Written on it were the words "Together in Paris." Would she ever remember who she was? Would she ever find her family?

Soon, Anya came to a crossroads. One road led to the Fisherman's Village, the other to St. Petersburg. Which way should she go? Anya glanced heavenward. "Send me a sign, a hint—anything!"

Just then, a small puppy ran up and grabbed the end of her scarf. He tugged her in the direction of St. Petersburg. This was her sign? A mutt?

"Oh, well," Anya laughed. In St. Petersburg, she could buy a ticket to Paris. Then maybe she could find her family. "Okay, little Pooka, show me the way!"

When they reached St. Petersburg, Anya learned that to buy a ticket to Paris, she needed travel papers. They were hard to get. "Psst!" an old woman whispered to her. "Go see Dimitri at the old palace."

The once-grand palace was now nothing more than a spooky ruin. Anya shivered as she stepped inside. "This place . . ." she whispered. "It's like a memory from a dream." As she closed her eyes, a song drifted through her mind. She remembered dancing, candlelight, someone tall and handsome holding her. . . .

"Hey!" came a voice. "What are you doing in here?"

$A$nya whirled around. Moonlight shone on her red hair and illuminated the painting behind her.

Dimitri gasped. The painting was of the Czar and his family. And Anya looked just like Anastasia!

"I need travel papers," she said, "to get to Paris."

Dimitri smiled. He'd found the actress to play the part of Anastasia. But he didn't tell her about the reward money. He told her that he and his friend Vladimir would take her to Paris to help her find her family. She might even *be* the missing Anastasia!

"You know, you do kind of resemble her . . ." Dimitri remarked.

"The same blue eyes . . . Nicholas's smile . . . oh, look, she even has the grandmother's hands!" exclaimed Vladimir.

"Me? Anastasia?" Anya thought they were crazy.

"Then again," Anya said, "if I don't remember who I am, then who's to say I'm *not* a duchess, right? Empress Marie will certainly know."

"Either way, it gets you to Paris!" Dimitri said.

Anya and Dimitri shook on it. Laughing, Dimitri shouted, "May I present Her Royal Highness, the Grand Duchess Anastasia!"

Up in the rafters a white bat nearly fell from his perch. "Anastasia?" Bartok gasped. "No, it can't be!"

He blew the dust off Rasputin's reliquary, and it came to life with an eerie green glow.

The reliquary took off like a wild horse, dragging Bartok down, down, deep into the earth. There he met Rasputin—half man, half spirit—and told him he'd found Anastasia.

"So that's why I'm stuck here in limbo," Rasputin growled. "My curse is unfulfilled! If only I hadn't lost the key to my powers!"

"You mean *this*?" Bartok held up the glowing reliquary.

Rasputin grabbed it in his rotting hands. "My destiny unfolds. Show me the little Romanov and—I swear—this time I will not fail!"

Anya, Dimitri, Vladimir, and Pooka settled into their train car as it chugged through the snowy countryside.

Just as the train guard began making his rounds, Vladimir discovered that the ink he'd used on their travel papers was the wrong color!

Quickly, Dimitri hustled them into the baggage car to hide.

It was crowded, dirty, and cold. But it was better than being thrown off the train in the middle of nowhere.

Tiny twisted creatures, Rasputin's minions, streaked through the dark night to surround the train. They crawled over the engine, making it speed faster and faster along the track. The smokestack glowed red and spouted ashes and sparks, and then *KABOOM!* The minions unhooked the engine and baggage car from the rest of the train.

The engine kept gaining speed. "Nobody's driving this train!" Dimitri cried. "We have to jump!" But they were flying along the edge of a cliff. "We'll unhook the baggage car from the engine!" Dimitri struck the coupling with a hammer, but the hammer broke.

Then Pooka and Anya discovered a box marked EXPLOSIVES. Anya reached inside, pulled out a stick of dynamite, lit it, and handed it to Dimitri.

Dimitri was impressed. "That'll work," he said, as he shoved it into the coupling.

*BOOM!* The front of the baggage car blew away, and the engine raced on without the rest of the car. Now it could coast to a stop.

But just ahead, the minions had destroyed the bridge. And the baggage car was rolling downhill straight for it.

Dimitri found a chain, hooked it to the bottom of the car, then threw the other end out the back. The hook worked like an anchor and jerked the car to a halt. Anya, Dimitri, Vladimir, and Pooka tumbled safely into a snowbank.

Beyond them, the engine ran off the broken bridge and plunged to the bottom of a gorge in a fiery crash.

The stranded group had to hike for days across the mountains to get to a port. On the way, Dimitri and Vladimir taught Anya manners, how to curtsy, and the names of all her royal relatives.

At last they boarded a ship and set sail for France. Dimitri surprised Anya with a beautiful new gown. Dimitri and Vladimir couldn't believe their eyes when Anya tried on the dress. They'd transformed a skinny tomboy into a grand duchess. She was beautiful!

Vladimir taught Anya and Dimitri how to waltz. As he watched them dance, Vladimir noticed something he hadn't seen before— Anya and Dimitri were falling in love!

TASHA TASHA TASHA

That night, as Anya slept, Rasputin sent his minions once more. Like smoky nightmares, they surrounded her.

Soon, Anya dreamed that she and her younger brother were playing in a field of butterflies. As the dream butterflies encircled her head, Anya rose from her bed. Sleepwalking, she followed them onto the upper deck of the ship.

Anya stood on a rock above a mountain pool. She watched her brother dive in. She saw her parents and sisters waving to her. "Jump!" her father called to her.

But that was only in the dream. She had really climbed over the railing of the ship. The minions swirled around her. Her father's face turned into one of the horrible creatures. "Jump!" it commanded.

Suddenly, hands grabbed her around the waist. Alerted by Pooka, Dimitri reached Anya just in time.

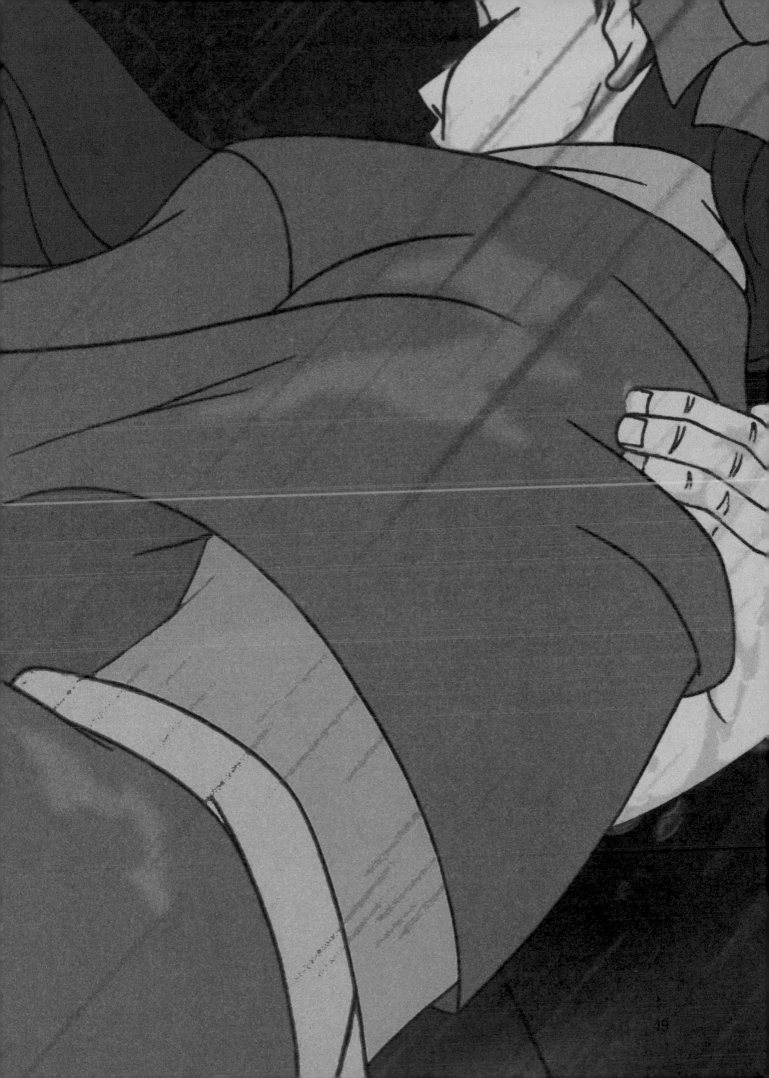

"Anya, Anya, wake up!" Dimitri cried.

Anya jolted awake. She threw her arms around Dimitri.

"It's all right," he whispered, holding her tight. "You're safe now."

But she wasn't safe. Deep in the underworld, Rasputin swore the girl would not escape him again.

In Paris, Empress Marie interviewed yet another girl who claimed to be her granddaughter. But she soon sent her away, just as she'd sent away all the others.

"I'm so sorry," said Marie's cousin Sophie as she added sugar to her cat's tea. "But we won't be fooled next time. I'm going to think of some really hard questions."

"No!" Marie said. "My heart can't take it anymore. I will see no more girls claiming to be Anastasia!"

That afternoon, Anya and her friends arrived in Paris, and Vladimir led them to Sophie's house. She was an old friend of his from Russia, and no one got near the Empress without convincing Sophie first.

Sophie smiled at Anya. "You certainly look like Anastasia! But tell me, dear, how did you escape from the palace?"

Anya was silent for a moment as a strange memory filled her head. "There was a boy who worked in the palace," she said softly. "He opened the wall and . . ." Then she laughed with embarrassment. "I'm sorry, that must sound crazy."

Dimitri stared at her. *He* had been that young boy. How could she remember something like that? Unless . . .

With a shock, he realized Anya really *was* Anastasia!

"So when do we see the Empress?" Vladimir asked.

"I'm afraid you don't," Sophie said. "She won't see any more girls."

"My dear Sophie," Vladimir said, "you *must* think of a way!"

Sophie thought for a moment, then smiled. "Do you like the Russian ballet? We simply *never* miss it!" she said with a wink.

That was it! They would try to see the Empress at the ballet.

That night, Anya, Dimitri, and Vladimir went to the ballet. Anya was so nervous, she could hardly watch the dancers.

Dimitri took her hand. "Everything's going to be fine," he assured her. But as he gazed into her beautiful blue eyes, he knew it wouldn't be fine for him. The Empress would recognize her granddaughter at once. Then Anya would walk out of his life forever.

A con artist from the streets was not fit for a grand duchess.

At intermission, they hurried to the Empress's box. Dimitri went in first to announce that he'd found Anastasia. But Marie refused to see her.

"Wait," he said. "My name is Dimitri. I used to work at the palace. And I tell you, this time it is really her!"

"Dimitri," Marie said, her eyes narrowing. "I've heard of you! You're that con man from St. Petersburg who was holding auditions to find an Anastasia look-alike! Remove him!"

"But she really is Anastasia!" Dimitri insisted. "If you'll only speak to her, you'll see!"

A guard threw Dimitri from the box. As soon as Dimitri saw Anya's face, he knew she'd heard everything.

"It was all a lie, wasn't it?" she whispered, devastated. "I thought you wanted to help me find my family. But you used me. I was just a part of your con game to get the Empress's money!"

Dimitri took her by the shoulders. "Anya, please—"

"No!" cried Anya, breaking free from his grasp. "Just leave me alone!" Then she ran from the opera house in tears.

Outside, Dimitri tricked Empress Marie's chauffeur, took his place, and drove the Empress to Sophie's house. "You have to talk to her!" he begged as he led her to the front door. "Please."

The Empress started to shove past him. Then he dug something from his pocket. "Do you recognize this?"

Marie froze. Trembling, she reached for the tiny music box. "Where did you get this?"

Dimitri opened the front door. "I know you've been hurt. But it's just possible that she's been as lost and alone as you."

Marie eyed him suspiciously, then entered the house.

$\mathcal{A}$nya was packing when she heard a knock at her door. She turned to find Empress Marie staring at her. "Who *are* you?" she asked Anya.

"I was hoping you could tell me," Anya answered.

Marie sighed. "My dear, I'm old and I'm tired of being tricked. You're a very good actress. But I've had enough." She swept past Anya to leave.

Anya sniffed the air. "Peppermint . . ."

The Empress paused, her hand upon the doorknob.

"It's an oil for my hands," Marie said.

Anya closed her eyes as the fragrance unlocked years of memories. "Yes," she whispered. "I spilled a bottle once. The carpet was soaked. And it forever smelled of peppermint." She opened her eyes. "Like you."

Marie saw the chain around Anya's neck. Slowly, she held out the music box. "This was our secret. Anastasia's and mine."

Anya wound the music box with her key. "The music box," she said, "to sing me to sleep when you were in Paris. . . ."

They stared at each other, then fell into each other's arms.

"My Anastasia!" Marie cried.

Their search was finally over.

The next day Marie sent for Dimitri. "The 10 million rubles are yours—as promised—with my gratitude."

But Dimitri no longer wanted the money. He wanted something that money could not buy.

"Young man, where did you get that music box?" Marie asked. When he didn't answer, she said, "You were the boy, weren't you? You saved her life, and mine. Now you've brought her to me, yet you want no reward. Why the change of mind?"

Dimitri simply bowed, then quickly left.

That night, Empress Marie held a ball to celebrate the return of her granddaughter. Anastasia peeked gloomily through a curtain at the couples waltzing around the room.

"Looking for someone?" Marie asked. "You know, your friend Dimitri—he refused to take the reward money."

Anastasia couldn't believe it—she had thought the money was all he ever wanted!

"You will have to decide what to do, my darling," Marie said. "There is no place for him out there in that glittering crowd, no place for him beside the Grand Duchess Anastasia. . . . But whatever you choose, I will hold you in my heart always."

$A$nastasia wondered what she would do if she had to choose between Dimitri and her crown. Suddenly she heard Pooka barking. She turned to see him disappearing through the terrace doors.

"Pooka?" Anastasia called, peering into the darkness. When he didn't answer, she hurried into the garden to find him.

$M$eanwhile, Dimitri stood in line at the train station, thinking about Anya . . . Anastasia . . . whatever her name was, he loved her.

"Tell her . . ." said a voice.

Someone poked him. "Where to, sir?" the ticket lady asked.

"Tell her!" the impatient man behind him repeated.

"I will!" Dimitri said. "I'll tell her I love her!"

The man and the ticket lady stared after him as Dimitri ran off, laughing madly, happily, in love.

In the garden, Anastasia searched for Pooka. She heard him bark and turned in his direction. But a tall bush blocked her path. Anastasia tried to find a different way out, but another bush appeared in front of her—she was trapped! Barking furiously at the surrounding shrubbery, Pooka ran up to her.

"An-a-sta-sia," a strange voice whispered.

Anastasia panicked. With Pooka at her heels, she ran through a small opening in the wall of bushes. On the other side, they stopped before a bridge. Someone was there, waiting for them.

"Your Imperial Highness," said the dark figure, bowing nastily. Anastasia gasped. He seemed so familiar. Anastasia tried desperately to remember who he was. She remembered a party . . . a curse. . . . Then the figure pointed his reliquary at her, and a blast of snow and ice knocked her to the ground! All at once, her memories came rushing back.

"Rasputin!" Anastasia cried. He had destroyed her family and her life ten years before. "I'm not afraid of you!"

"I can fix that," he said. With an evil laugh, Rasputin pointed the reliquary at Anastasia once again. Swarms of minions flew at Anastasia and pushed her over the side of the bridge.

"Say your prayers, Anastasia!" Rasputin cackled as he watched her struggling not to fall into the icy river. "No one can save you!"

"Wanna bet?" Dimitri asked, charging at Rasputin. Rasputin blasted Dimitri to the ground. Then Rasputin peered over the side of the bridge, looking for Anastasia, and saw nothing but a cloud of ice and smoke. His curse had worked at last—finally, the last Romanov was gone!

"Long live the Romanovs!" he shrieked sarcastically.

"*I* couldn't have said it better myself," replied Anastasia, stepping through the smoke. She confronted Rasputin. As they struggled, Pooka leaped up and grabbed the reliquary in his mouth. Then he dropped it at Anastasia's feet.

Rasputin cowered. He was helpless without his reliquary, the source of all his power!

"This is for Dimitri!" Anastasia said, stomping on the reliquary.

"This is for my family!" she added, stepping on it again.

"And this is for you!" she shouted as the reliquary finally broke.

"AAAGGGHHH!" Rasputin screamed. Hundreds of minions, now released from captivity, streamed out of the reliquary. Anastasia watched as the minions surrounded Rasputin, their wings beating him down, until she could no longer see him.

When the minions flew away a few seconds later, Rasputin was gone forever.

Anastasia hurried over to Dimitri and gently stroked his hair. At her touch, he began to wake up. They were both so relieved to see each other, they couldn't hide their feelings any longer.

"You didn't take the money," Anastasia said.

"I couldn't . . ." he replied.

Anastasia knew he felt the same way about her as she did about him. They moved closer together, about to embrace, when Pooka barked and trotted over to them.

Pooka had brought them Anastasia's crown, which had fallen off during her struggle with Rasputin. Slowly, Dimitri took it from Pooka and held it out to Anastasia.

"They're waiting for you," Dimitri reminded her.

Anastasia looked from Dimitri to the crown and back again. The time had come to make a choice.

Later that night at the palace, the butler brought a package to Empress Marie. Surprised, she opened it, then smiled a bittersweet smile. Anastasia had returned her crown.

Sophie wiped her eyes. "It seems like only yesterday she came here!" she said.

"At least we had that yesterday," Marie replied. "Now she has her tomorrow."

Under the starry sky, Anastasia and Dimitri embraced. They both knew they were exactly where they wanted to be. Home could be anywhere, as long as they were together.